WALT DISNEY PRESENTS # Tigger
and Winnie-the-Pooh

Pictures by the Walt Disney Studio

 GOLDEN PRESS
Western Publishing Company, Inc.
Racine, Wisconsin

Eighteenth Printing, 1982

Bounce, bounce! Here comes Tigger
to visit Winnie-the-Pooh.

"It's going to be a Blustery Day," says Tigger. But Winnie-the-Pooh just goes on eating honey.

Tigger goes to tell Kanga and Roo, "We're going to have a Blustery Day."

Then Tigger stays
to have a taste of Roo's
strengthening syrup.

Here come the wind and rain!
No more thistles for Eeyore; it's
time for him to go home now.

Poor Eeyore!
His house is floating away!

Piglet's house is surrounded
by water, so he puts a message—
Help!—into a bottle and
tosses it from his window.

Christopher Robin finds Piglet's
note in the bottle.

Owl flies off to look for Piglet.

Winnie-the-Pooh and Christopher Robin
set out in a wobbly umbrella-boat
to rescue Piglet.

Soon Winnie-the-Pooh and Christopher Robin reach Piglet's house. Owl is there, too.

The friends sail to shore together
in their Blustery-Day boat. Everyone
is so very happy to see them!

Piglet and Pooh celebrate the rescue
with a little something to eat.